An Aesop's Fable

Retold by Elsie Nelley   Illustrations by Mehrdokht Amini

Contents

Chapter 1

A Problem

One day, a long time ago, the Wind said to the Sun, "I am so strong, I can rip huge trees out of the ground and make the roofs of houses fly up into the air."

The Sun thought for a moment, and then said,
“But I am strong, too. I can melt ice and turn it into water.
And in summer, the fields are brown.
I make them change colour.”

"But that doesn't mean you are stronger than me," cried the Wind. "I can make waves as high as mountains! I am so strong I can blow sailing boats up onto the land. People feel afraid and stay inside when I turn into a storm."

"That may be so," said the Sun quietly,
"but without me there would be no life on Earth."

Just then, the Sun looked down on the town and noticed a young man walking along a path.

"Wind, do you see that man down there, walking along slowly, wearing a heavy coat and warm hat?" asked the Sun.
"Let's see which one of us is able to make him take off his coat.
Then we will know who is stronger."

"That's a good idea," said the Wind.
"I'll go first. This will be so easy for me."

Chapter 2

The Wind Goes First

The Wind huffed and puffed and huffed and puffed. Leaves blew off the trees. Clouds sped across the sky. Umbrellas were blown inside out.

The young man put a hand up to hold his hat in place, but he was too late.
The Wind had already tossed it up into the air.

The man turned up the collar of his coat
and pulled it tighter around himself.
"What's happened to the weather?" he thought.
"Suddenly, it is so windy, I can hardly stand up."

The Wind was disappointed because he hadn't been able to make the man take off his coat.

"Sun, are you watching?" cried the Wind. "This time I'll get the man to take off his coat!"

The Wind whistled and roared.
Doors slammed and windows shook.
But the young man only pulled his coat
more tightly around himself and hurried down the path.

"Oh, dear!" groaned the Wind. "Look at him!
He's still wearing his coat!"

"Yes," grinned the Sun. "It must be my turn now."

Chapter 3

The Sun's Turn

The Sun shone down gently on the man and spread sunlight all around. The sky turned blue again and the air became warm.

"What a strange day it is today," said the young man. "It's freezing one minute and warm the next." So he stopped and began to undo the buttons on his coat.

The young man looked around for a shady tree where he could rest for a moment.

The Sun grew brighter and brighter.

“It’s like a summer’s day,” the young man thought. “I will have to take off my coat.”

Chapter 4

Who Is Stronger?

The Sun was delighted.

"Wind, look what the young man is doing," the Sun cried. "He's taking off his coat! I've won!"

The Wind was surprised.
"Why couldn't I get him to take off his coat?" he asked.
"I thought I was much stronger than you."

"You tried very hard," the Sun said kindly. "But today, it was better to be gentle and warm than too big and strong."